The Hole in the Garden

Written by Jill Eggleton
Illustrated by John Bennett

Rigby

One day, Eddy saw a
big hole in the garden.
"Who made that
big hole?" he said.

Eddy's dad looked
at the hole.
He looked and looked.
"I can't see who
made it," he said.

Eddy went to school
and he wrote a story.

The teacher liked
Eddy's story.
She put it on the wall.

The next day,
the hole was **bigger**.
Eddy showed the hole
to his dad again.

His dad looked and
looked at the hole.
"I can't see who made
this hole," he said.

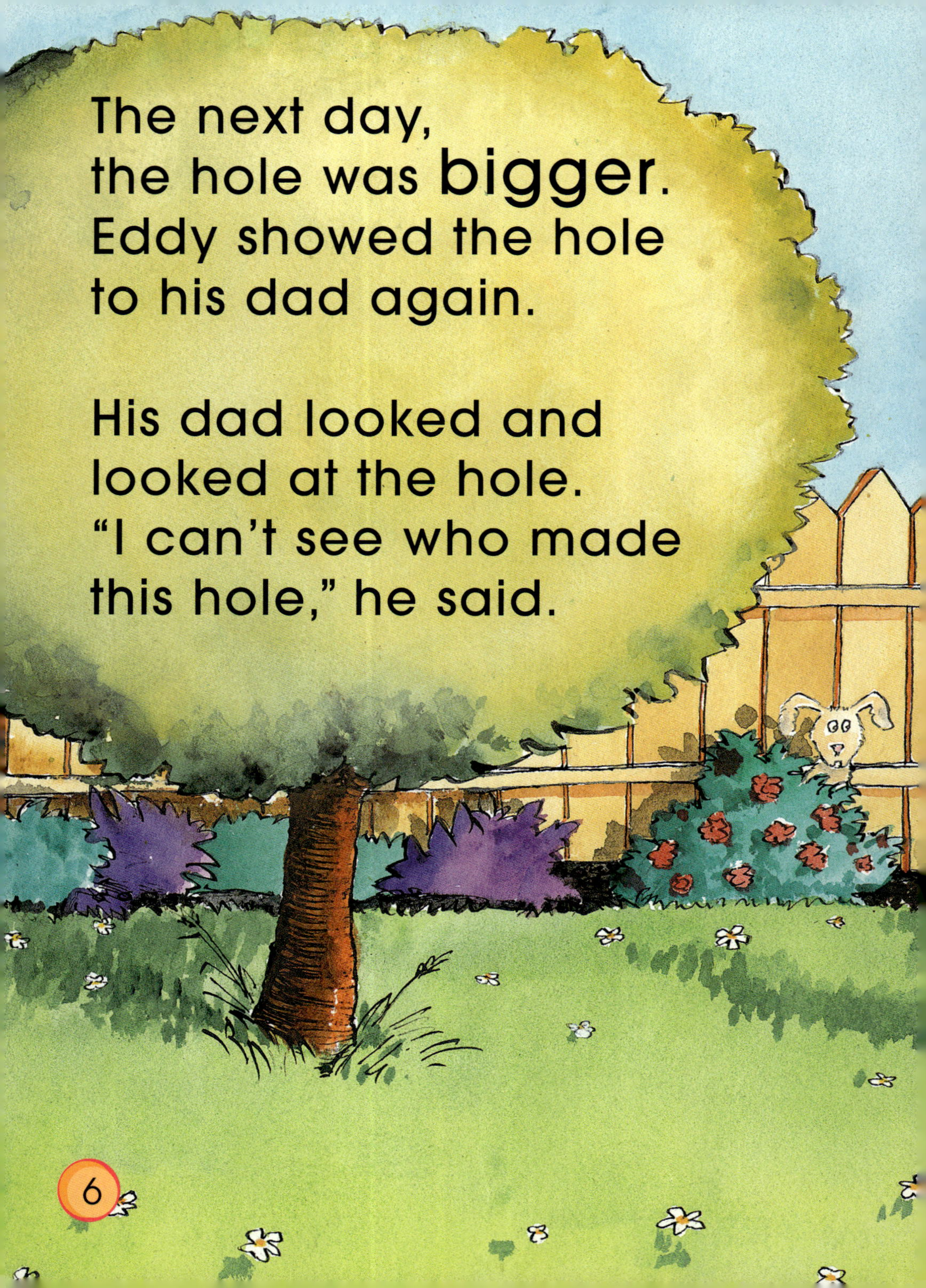

Eddy went to school
and he wrote a story.

The teacher liked
this story, too.
She put it on the wall.

The next day,
a woman came
to look at the hole.
She had a computer
and a camera.

“**Look**,” she said.
“Rabbits have made
this big hole.”

Eddy went to school
and he wrote a story.

The teacher
put Eddy's story
on the wall again.

The Hole
Last night, giants came and sat in the yard. They had a picnic and they made a very big hole.
By Eddy
The Hole
A woman came to our house. She had a computer. She looked under the ground with the camera and I saw rabbits on the computer.
By Eddy

The kids read Eddy's stories.
"Wow!" they said.
"Eddy can make up
good stories."

A True or False Chart

Is this
True or False?

Is this
True or False?

Is this
True or False?

Guide Notes

Title: The Hole in the Garden

Stage: Early (3) – Blue

Genre: Fiction

Approach: Guided Reading

Processes: Thinking Critically, Exploring Language, Processing Information

Written and Visual Focus: True or False Chart, Thought Bubbles

THINKING CRITICALLY

(sample questions)

- What do you think this story could be about?
- Focus on the title and discuss.
- Look at pages 2-3 and 6-7. Why do you think Eddy's dad couldn't see who made the hole?
- Look at pages 4 and 8. Where do you think Eddy got the ideas for his stories?
- Look at pages 5, 9 and 13. Why do you think the teacher liked Eddy's stories?
- Look at pages 10 and 11. How do you think the woman could see the rabbits on the computer?

EXPLORING LANGUAGE

Terminology

Title, cover, illustrations, author, illustrator

Vocabulary

Interest words: computer, camera, wrote
High-frequency words (new): who, next
Positional words: on, in, under

Print Conventions

Capital letter for sentence beginnings and names (**E**ddy), periods, commas, quotation marks, question marks, exclamation marks